The Mystery of
The Locked Door

by Dan Cohen • *Pictures by* George Overlie

CAROLRHODA BOOKS
MINNEAPOLIS, MINNESOTA U.S.A.

1 2 3 4 5 6 7 8 9 10 85 84 83 82 81 80 79

"This has got to be the most puzzling crime that has ever been committed in Spring Grove," said Officer Grover Greenwood.

He was sitting with his two special friends, Ruthann and her little sister, Polly, in the Spring Grove Ice Cream Shop. They often met there for a treat. The Ice Cream Shop was where Officer Greenwood got some of his best ideas about his cases. There was something about a banana split, topped with lots of whipped cream and a cherry, that helped him think.

Officer Greenwood patted his large waistline. "Just as soon as I solve this case, I'll go back on my diet," he said. "But solving it won't be easy. In fact, maybe you girls can help. The case involves a coin collection. Ruthann, I understand you're quite a collector yourself."

"Well, I *do* have a nice collection of Lincoln pennies," said Ruthann.

"And she's always reading books about coins," said Polly.

"Well, if you two can help me solve this case, I'll buy you both a super-deluxe banana split every week for a month," said Officer Greenwood. "Here are the facts. Just last year, Mr. Barber started to collect coins. He's very wealthy, and in a short time he had quite a valuable collection."

"Gee, did he keep it in a safe?" asked Polly.
"No," said Officer Greenwood. "But he kept
it in his study with the door locked at all times.

There is only one key to the door. And the window is locked from the inside. But somehow a thief broke in last night. He made the mistake of flashing a light, and the next-door

neighbor saw it. The neighbor dashed over to
the house to tell the caretaker. When they got
to the study, the door was locked! By the time
they could break in, the thief had disappeared.

And with him had gone the best coin in the whole collection. It was one of the first silver dollars made in the United States. It's worth thousands of dollars." Officer Greenwood sighed. "I tell you, this is one mystery I just can't figure out."

"Who had the key, Officer Greenwood?" asked Ruthann.

"Mr. Barber, that's who," said Officer Greenwood. "At first I thought he might have tried to steal his own coin to collect the insurance. But there *was* no insurance. Mr. Barber can even prove he was out of town when the coin was taken." Officer Greenwood finished his banana split and loosened his belt a little.

"Well, I'm going to go over to Mr. Barber's house and question the caretaker again," he said. "On the way, I'll give you girls a ride home in the police car if you like."

"Can we go with you to Mr. Barber's?" Ruthann asked.

"Well, I really shouldn't take you along on police work," said Officer Greenwood. "But I suppose it can't hurt this once."

When they got to Mr. Barber's house, Homer
Humphrey, the caretaker, met them at the door.
He took them to his tiny room at the back of
the house.

"When Mr. Barber's not home, I sleep in the room next to where he keeps those coins," he said nervously. "I don't know how I missed hearing the thief in the next room. But I had just gone to sleep when I heard a whole lot of noise at the front door. Somebody whoopin' and

a hollerin'. When I got there it was old Mr. Grimsby from next door. Never seen him so excited. He said he saw a light coming from inside the study. Said that could only mean there was somebody in there. He said he ran right over instead of taking time to call the police."

"What happened then?" asked Officer Greenwood.

"Well, we broke down the door. But by the time we got in, the thief had gotten away somehow. I checked the window latch, but no one had touched it. There were no marks on the door lock either. I just don't know how the thief got in. Mr. Grimsby checked the closet shelf on the other side of the room, where Mr. Barber kept his coins. He wanted to see if anything was missing. He gave out one of those whoops of his when he saw it."

"Saw what?" asked Officer Greenwood.

"An empty space where a coin was missing. Mr. Barber liked to keep them in neat little rows, all polished up like bright silver buttons.

He liked to take them out and look at them.
But there was a space in the row where the
silver dollar had been. It was gone!"

"How long have you worked for Mr. Barber, Homer?" asked Officer Greenwood.

"Twenty years," said Homer.

"That's certainly plenty of time to make an extra key, isn't it? Then Mr. Barber just happened to go on a nice, long trip . . ."

"Yes, but . . ."

"Officer Greenwood?"

"What is it, Ruthann?"

"We've got to go now. Mom and Dad will be awfully mad if we're late for dinner," said Ruthann. "We'll just take the bus. It goes right by here." She handed the caretaker a fifty-cent piece. "Mr. Humphrey, could you give me change for bus fare?"

"I guess so," said Homer. He reached in his pocket and handed over the change. Then he absent-mindedly stuffed the fifty-cent piece in his pocket. He turned back to Officer Greenwood. "I'm not a thief," said Homer.

"Maybe not," said Officer Greenwood. "But I'd just as soon you didn't leave town for a little while, until this matter gets worked out."

The girls had just gotten to the front door when Officer Greenwood caught up with them.

"Hold on—I can't have you running off by yourselves in a strange neighborhood," he said.

"You know, that was very interesting," said Ruthann. "I guess Mr. Barber *is* new at collecting coins. I've read that experienced collectors never polish their coins. By the way, can we go with you when you visit Mr. Grimsby tomorrow?"

"What makes you think I'm going to do that?" asked Officer Greenwood.

"Because I think Homer Humphrey is telling the truth," said Ruthann. Then she whispered something in Officer Greenwood's ear, and he winked and nodded.

The next day after school, Officer Greenwood picked up the girls in his police car. They went to see Mr. Grimsby. He wasn't at all nervous. His story of what had happened was very much like Homer's. He showed them where he had been standing when he saw the light in Mr. Barber's study. "I know it looks bad for Homer," said Mr. Grimsby. "But I really don't think he did it, even though he did need money."

"What do you mean?" asked Officer Green-wood.

"Oops! Maybe I said something I shouldn't have. It's just that I heard Homer was having trouble making ends meet."

"Are you a coin collector, Mr. Grimsby?" asked Officer Greenwood.

"I thought you'd get around to that, Officer. Yes, I am. As a matter of fact, it is well known that I have some very fine coins myself. Of course, I had heard about Mr. Barber's new collection. Everyone had. That's why I looked for the silver dollar when we finally got in the room. I was afraid that would be exactly what the thief would be after. You see, I have one of the best examples of that coin in the world. Far finer than Mr. Barber's. Of course, I've owned it for over twenty years. Things were a little cheaper when I bought it. Heh, heh."

"May we see it?" asked Officer Greenwood.

"I haven't had that silver dollar out of the safe for many, many years, Officer. I'm afraid not."

"Oh, please show it to us, Mr. Grimsby," said Ruthann. "I'd love to see it. I'm a coin collector just like you."

"Might be nice, Mr. Grimsby," said Officer Greenwood.

"Oh, all right," said Mr. Grimsby.

In a few minutes, he was back with the coin.
"It sure is bright and shiny," said Polly.

"That's right, Polly. That's why I don't think Mr. Grimsby is telling the truth," said Officer Greenwood.

"What are you talking about, Greenwood?" asked Mr. Grimsby.

"If you had left that coin in your safe for many years, Mr. Grimsby, it wouldn't be so bright and shiny," said Officer Greenwood. "Unless silver is polished, it tarnishes, or gets dark, after a time. Ruthann tells me that most experienced collectors like you would never polish their fine coins, even though they did get dark. But this coin has just been polished. Mr. Barber was new at coin collecting. He liked his coins polished like buttons in a row. This is Mr. Barber's missing coin!"

"How could I have old Barber's coin? That room was locked!" said Mr. Grimsby.

"It was locked until you and Homer broke down the door. There never was any light in the study. You just made that up so you could get into the room. While Homer was busy looking for signs of the thief, you stole the coin," said Officer Greenwood.

Mr. Grimsby didn't say much after that. He said even less when Officer Greenwood took him down to the police station to be booked for stealing the silver dollar.

The next day, Officer Greenwood met Ruthann and Polly at the Spring Grove Ice Cream
Shop. They had helped solve the mystery of
the locked room. Now they were enjoying their
rewards—two super-deluxe banana splits.

"How did you know that Homer was telling
the truth, Ruthann?" asked Polly.

"When I asked Homer to change my half dollar, he didn't even look at it," said Ruthann. "Anyone who's interested in coins always looks at half dollars. That's because you don't see many of them anymore. I just don't think Homer knew enough about coins to have even known which one to take. And the only coin missing was the most valuable coin in the collection."

She turned to Officer Greenwood. "How did you know that Mr. Grimsby was lying about the light in the study?" she asked.

"Well, there wasn't any way for anyone to get into that room until Homer and Mr. Grimsby broke down the door. So Grimsby had to have made up the story about the light," said Officer Greenwood. "Then, Ruthann, what you told me about polishing coins helped me to figure out the rest."

"You sure are smart," said Polly.

"Well, thank you, Polly. Did you enjoy your banana split?"

"I sure did, and I can hardly wait until next week," said Polly. "And the week after that, and then the week after that."

"What do you mean, Polly?" asked Officer Greenwood.

"Don't you remember?" teased Ruthann. "You said that if we helped solve the case, you would buy us banana splits for a whole month!"

"I'm afraid you're right, girls," said Officer Greenwood, sighing. "Well, there goes another diet!"